Day and Night Nursery Rhymes

Best of Mother Goose Treasures

Illustrated by Svitlana Gorpinchenko

For both children and adults, for kids and parents who will enjoy the lively language of subtle folk humor and the elegant style of the genuine children's nursery rhymes.

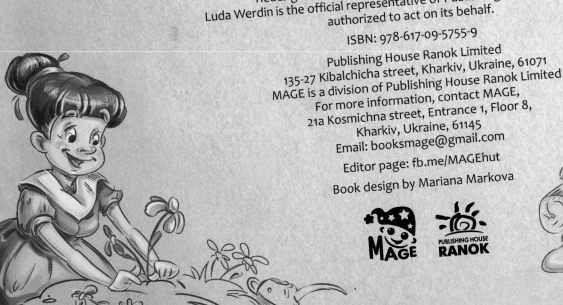

MAGE

Day and Night Nursery Rhymes

Best of Mother Goose Treasures

Created in 2016 by MAGE team.
First published in 2016 by Publishing House Ranok Limited.

Redesigned for global publishing by Luda Werdin in 2019.
Luda Werdin is the official representative of Publishing House Ranok Limited authorized to act on its behalf.

ISBN: 978-617-09-5755-9

Publishing House Ranok Limited
135-27 Kibalchicha street, Kharkiv, Ukraine, 61071
MAGE is a division of Publishing House Ranok Limited
For more information, contact MAGE,
21a Kosmichna street, Entrance 1, Floor 8,
Kharkiv, Ukraine, 61145
Email: booksmage@gmail.com

Editor page: fb.me/MAGEhut

Book design by Mariana Markova

Contents

Day and Night

Day and night,
Sun and moon,
Air and light
Everyone must have,
And none can buy.

Fingers and Toes

Every baby in this land
Has twenty nails, upon each hand,
Five, and twenty on hands and feet:
All this is true, without deceit.

Days of the Month

Thirty days hath September,
April, June, and November;
All the rest have thirty-one
Except for February alone,
Which has twenty-eight each year,
Twenty-nine each Leap Year.

The Seasons

Spring is showery, flowery, bowery,
Summer is hoppy, croppy, poppy,
Autumn is wheezy, sneezy, freezy,
Winter is slippy, drippy, nippy.

One Misty, Moisty Morning

One misty, moisty morning,
When cloudy was the weather,
There I met an old man
All clothed in leather,
All clothed in leather,
With a cap under his chin.
How do you do?
And how do you do?
And how do you do again?

Sam, Sam, the Dirty Man

Sam, Sam, the dirty man,
Washed his face in a frying pan,
And combed his hair
With a leg of a chair,
And told his wife
He didn't really care.

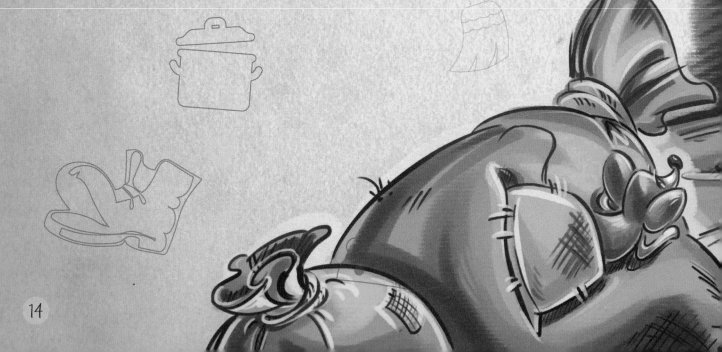

One, Two, Three, Four, Five

One, Two, Three, Four, Five,
Once I caught a fish alive,
Six, Seven, Eight, Nine, Ten,
Then I threw him back again.
Why did you let him go?
Because he bit my finger so.
Which finger did he bite?
This little finger on my right.

Little Jack Horner

Little Jack Horner
Sat in the corner,
Eating a Christmas pie;
He put in his thumb,
And pulled out a plum,
And said, "What
a good boy am I!"

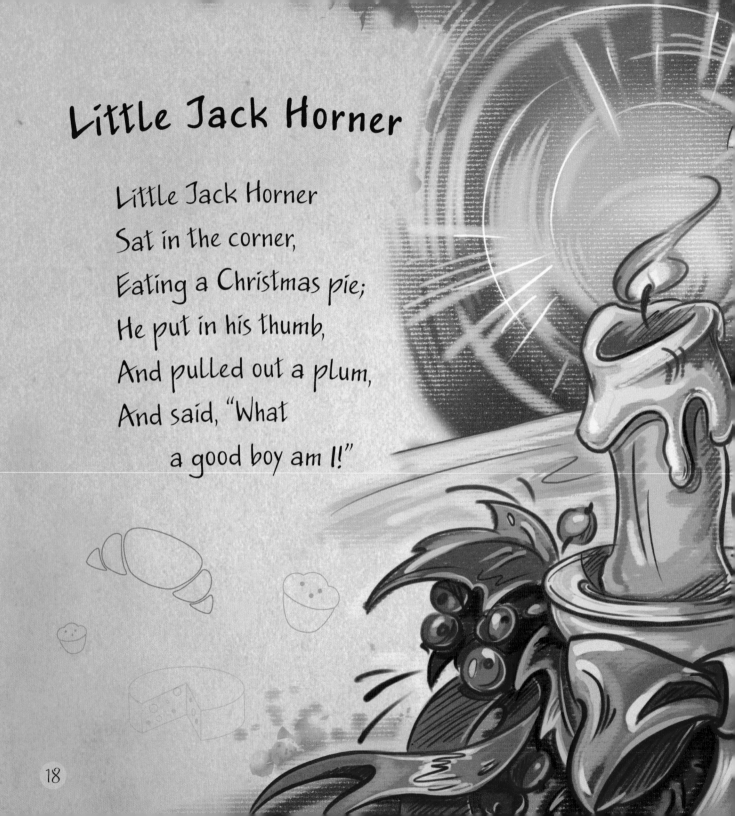

Jerry Hall

Jerry Hall,
He is so small,
A rat could eat him,
Hat and all.

Five Fat Sausages

Five fat sausages frying in a pan,
All of a sudden one went BANG!
Four fat sausages...
Three fat sausages...
Two fat sausages...
One fat sausage...
Then there were NO Sausages left!

23

Baa, Baa, Black Sheep

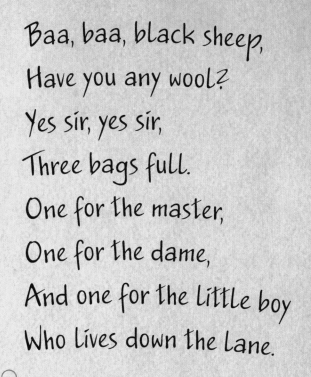

Baa, baa, black sheep,
Have you any wool?
Yes sir, yes sir,
Three bags full.
One for the master,
One for the dame,
And one for the little boy
Who lives down the lane.

I Love Little Pussy

I love little pussy,
Her coat is so warm,
And if I don't hurt her,
She'll do me no harm.
So I'll not pull her tail,
Nor drive her away,
But pussy and I

Very gently will play.
She shall sit by my side,
And I'll give her some food;
And pussy will love me
Because I am good.

There Was an Old Woman

There was an old woman
Lived under a hill,
She put a mouse in a bag,
And sent it to the mill.
The miller did swear,
By point of his knife,
He never took toll
Of a mouse in his life.

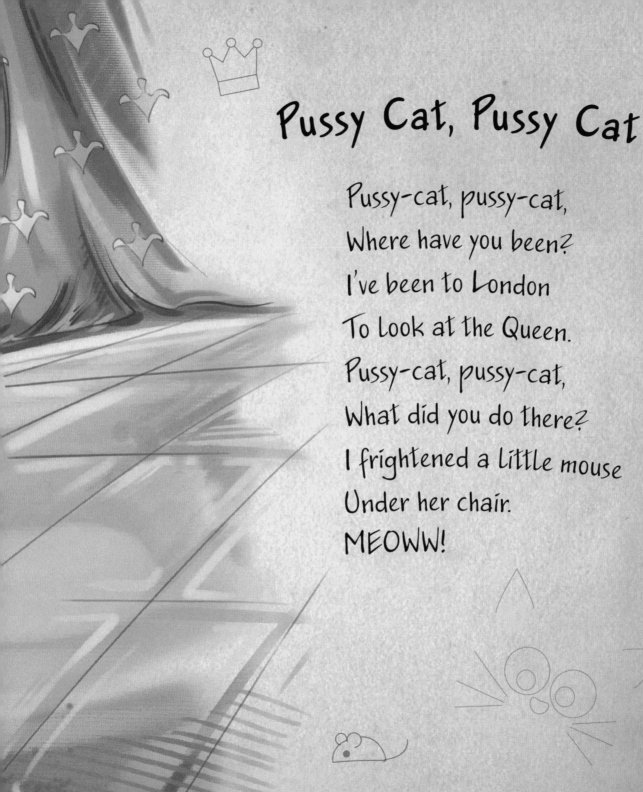

Pussy Cat, Pussy Cat

Pussy-cat, pussy-cat,
Where have you been?
I've been to London
To look at the Queen.
Pussy-cat, pussy-cat,
What did you do there?
I frightened a little mouse
Under her chair.
MEOWW!

The Itsy Bitsy Spider

The itsy-bitsy spider
Crawled up the water spout.
Down came the rain,
And washed the spider out.
Out came the sun,
And dried up all the rain,
And the itsy-bitsy spider
Went up the spout again.

The North Wind Doth Blow

The north wind doth blow,
And we shall have snow,
And what will poor robin
Do then?
Poor thing,
He'll sit in a barn,
And keep himself warm,
And hide his head
Under his wing,
Poor thing.

Ladybird! Ladybird!

Ladybird, ladybird,
Fly away home,
Your house is on fire
And your children all gone;
All except one
And that's little Ann,
And she has crept under
The warming pan.

Bat, Bat,
Come under My Hat

Bat, bat, come under my hat,

And I'll give you a slice of bacon;

And when I bake,

I'll give you a cake,

If I'm not mistaken.

Once I Saw a Little Bird

Once I saw a little bird
Come hop, hop, hop;
So I cried, "Little bird,
Will you stop, stop, stop?"
I was going to the window,
To say, "How do you do?"
But he shook his little tail,
And far away he flew.

A Wise Old Owl

A wise old owl sat in an oak,
The more he heard the less he spoke;
The less he spoke the more he heard.
Why aren't we all like that
Wise old bird?

Mother Goose Nursery Rhymes. A collection of stories called "Mother Goose's Tales" was published in 1729, and the first confirmed collection of Nursery Rhymes using the term "Mother Goose" was published in 1780. The *Mother Goose* brand caught the imagination of publishers and the population. The origin of the name *Mother Goose* is unclear though there have been various claims for it. The illustrations accompanying the publications invariably depicted 'Mother Goose' as an old crone or a witch.

MAGE is a creative team of professional authors, artists, and child psychologists, which within the period of 15 years has created more than 5000 books, games, and collections of instructional tasks for children. Enjoyable yet engaging and educational books are the goal of "MAGE". Currently, the "MAGE" team is located in Ukraine and is carrying out the work on children's books projects.

Svitlana Gorpinchenko is known for her funny and colorful illustrations for a lot of children's books. Her works, filled with love for the world around, are full of humor and interesting composition layout. She currently lives with her favorite cat, keeping her work on new illustrations.

Thank you for choosing our book!

You can always find an up-to-date list of the titles of this series as well as our other books, on our **FB** page: fb.me/MAGEhut

Subscribe to it! Be the first to know when we have a new release! Sign up for our page to get newsletters. We only post when we have book news — it is true!

Share it! If you enjoyed this book, please lend your copy to a friend who might enjoy it, too.

Review it! Please consider posting a short book review. Honest reader impressions help other people decide whether they might enjoy the book and make the right choice!

Create with us! We'd love to hear from you! Stop by our Facebook page to discuss updates, illustrations, and cover reveals, or just to spend time together!

Love, MAGE team

Also by MAGE

Enjoy wonderfully illustrated Rudyard Kipling's stories:

 Rikki Tikki Tavi: The Jungle Book Stories

 The Cat That Walked by Himself. How the Rhinoceros Got His Skin

 How the Leopard Got His Spots. The Beginning of the Armadillos

 The Elephant's Child. How the Camel Got His Hump

Spend the time of your life with your child enjoying this collection of magnificently illustrated best-loved nursery rhymes:

 Twinkle, Twinkle, Little Star: Colorful Nursery Rhymes

Learn about the world around with My First Picturepedias:

My Animal
Picturepedia

My Cozy Home
Picturepedia

Polite
Manners
Picturepedia

Health and Safety
Picturepedia

Immerse yourself in the miracle world of creativity and fantasy of the mage artist and the genius poet with the My Wondrous World art book:

My Wondrous World:
Rhymed Paintings and
Painted Rhymes